VIOLET STR

The Second Bullet

ANNA KATHARINE GREEN

PROBLEM 2

first published in 1915

"No. No."

"She's a most unhappy woman. Husband and child both taken from her in a moment; and now, all means of living as well, unless some happy thought of yours—some inspiration of your genius—shows us a way of re-establishing her claims to the policy voided by this cry of suicide."

But the small wise head of Violet Strange continued its slow shake of decided refusal.

"I'm sorry," she protested, "but it's quite out of my province. I'm too young to meddle with so serious a matter."

"Not when

you can save a bereaved woman the only possible compensation left her by untoward fate?"

"Let the police try their hand at that."

"They have had no success with the case."

"Or you?"

"Nor I either."

"And you expect—"

"Yes, Miss Strange. I expect you to find the missing bullet which will settle the fact that murder and not suicide ended George Hammond's life. If you cannot, then a long litigation awaits this poor widow, ending, as such litigation usually does, in favour of the stronger party. There's the alternative. If you once saw her—"

"But that's what I'm not willing to do. If I once saw her I should yield to her importunities and attempt the seemingly impossible. My instincts bid me say no. Give me something easier."

"Easier things are not so remunerative. There's money in this affair, if the

insurance company
is forced to pay up. I
can offer you—"

"What?"

There was eagerness
in the tone
despite her effort
at nonchalance.
The other smiled
imperceptibly, and
briefly named the
sum.

It was larger than
she had expected.

This her visitor saw by the way her eyelids fell and the peculiar stillness which, for an instant, held her vivacity in check.

"And you think I can earn that?"

Her eyes were fixed on his in an eagerness as honest as it was unrestrained.

He could hardly conceal his amazement, her desire was so evident and the cause of it so difficult to understand. He knew she wanted money—that was her avowed reason for entering into this uncongenial work. But to want it so much! He glanced at her person; it was simply clad but very expensively—how

expensively it was
his business to know.
Then he took in the
room in which they
sat. Simplicity again,
but the simplicity
of high art—the
drawing-room of
one rich enough to
indulge in the final
luxury of a highly
cultivated taste,
viz.: unostentatious
elegance and the
subjection of each
carefully chosen

ornament to the general effect.

What did this favoured child of fortune lack that she could be reached by such a plea, when her whole being revolted from the nature of the task he offered her? It was a question not new to him; but one he had never heard answered and was not likely to hear answered now. But the fact remained that the consent he had thought dependent upon sympathetic interest could be reached much more readily by the promise of large emolument,—and he owned to a feeling of secret disappointment even while he recognized the value of the discovery.

But his satisfaction in the latter, if satisfaction it were, was of very short duration. Almost immediately he observed a change in her. The sparkle which had shone in the eye whose depths he had never been able to penetrate, had dissipated itself in something like a tear and she spoke up in that vigorous tone no one but himself had ever heard, as she said:

"No. The sum is a good one and I could use it; but I will not waste my energy on a case I do not believe in. The man shot himself. He was a speculator, and probably had good reason for his act. Even his wife acknowledges that he has lately had more losses than gains."

"See her. She has something to tell you which never got into the papers."

"You say that? You know that?"

"On my honour, Miss Strange."

Violet pondered; then suddenly succumbed.

"Let her come, then. Prompt to the hour. I will receive her at three. Later I have a tea and two party calls to make."

Her visitor rose to leave. He had been able to subdue all evidence of his extreme gratification, and now took on a formal air. In dismissing a guest, Miss Strange was invariably the society belle and that only. This he had come to recognize.

The case (well known at the time) was, in the fewest possible words, as follows:

On a sultry night in September, a young couple living in one of the large apartment houses in

the extreme upper
portion of Manhattan
were so annoyed
by the incessant
crying of a child in
the adjoining suite,
that they got up, he
to smoke, and she
to sit in the window
for a possible breath
of cool air. They
were congratulating
themselves upon
the wisdom they
had shown in thus
giving up all thought

of sleep—for the child's crying had not ceased—when (it may have been two o'clock and it may have been a little later) there came from somewhere near, the sharp and somewhat peculiar detonation of a pistol-shot.

He thought it came from above; she, from the rear, and

they were staring at each other in the helpless wonder of the moment, when they were struck by the silence. The baby had ceased to cry. All was as still in the adjoining apartment as in their own—too still—much too still. Their mutual stare turned to one of horror. "It came from there!" whispered the wife. "Some accident has occurred to Mr. or Mrs. Hammond—we ought to go—"

Her words—very tremulous ones—were broken by a shout from below. They were standing in their window and had evidently been seen by a passing policeman. "Anything wrong up there?" they heard him cry. Mr. Saunders immediately looked out. “Nothing wrong here,” he called down. (They were but two stories from the pavement.) “But I’m not so sure about the rear apartment. We thought we heard a shot. Hadn’t you better come up, officer? My wife is nervous about it. I’ll meet you at the stair-head and show you the way.”

The officer nodded and stepped in. The young couple hastily donned some wraps, and, by the time he appeared on their floor, they were ready to accompany him.

Meanwhile, no disturbance was apparent anywhere else in the house, until the policeman rang the bell of the

Hammond apartment. Then, voices began to be heard, and doors to open above and below, but not the one before which the policeman stood.

Another ring, and this time an insistent one;—and still no response. The officer's hand was rising for the third time when there came a sound

of fluttering from
behind the panels
against which he
had laid his ear, and
finally a choked voice
uttering unintelligible
words. Then a hand
began to struggle
with the lock, and
the door, slowly
opening, disclosed
a woman clad in
a hastily donned
wrapper and giving
every evidence of
extreme fright.

"Oh!" she exclaimed, seeing only the compassionate faces of her neighbours. "You heard it, too! a pistol-shot from there—there—my husband's room. I have not dared to go—I—I—O, have mercy and see if anything is wrong! It is so still—so still, and only a moment ago the baby was crying. Mrs. Saunders,

Mrs. Saunders, why is it so still?”

She had fallen into her neighbour’s arms. The hand with which she had pointed out a certain door had sunk to her side and she appeared to be on the verge of collapse.

The officer eyed her sternly, while noting her appearance, which was that of a woman hastily risen from bed.

"Where were you?" he asked. "Not with your husband and child, or you would know what had happened there."

"I was sleeping down the hall," she managed to gasp out. "I'm not well—I—Oh, why do you all stand still and do nothing? My baby's in there.

Go! go!" and, with sudden energy, she sprang upright, her eyes wide open and burning, her small well featured face white as the linen she sought to hide.

The officer demurred no longer. In another instant he was trying the door at which she was again pointing.

It was locked.

Glancing back at the woman, now cowering almost to the floor, he pounded at the door and asked the man inside to open.

No answer came back.

With a sharp turn he glanced again at the wife.

“You say that your husband is in this room?”

She nodded, gasping faintly, "And the child!"

He turned back, listened, then beckoned to Mr. Saunders. "We shall have to break our way in," said he. "Put your shoulder well to the door. Now!"

The hinges of the door creaked; the lock gave way (this special officer

weighed two hundred
and seventy-five, as
he found out, next
day), and a prolonged
and sweeping crash
told the rest.

Mrs. Hammond gave
a low cry; and,
straining forward
from where she
crouched in terror on
the floor, searched
the faces of the two
men for some hint of
what they saw in the

dimly-lighted space beyond. Something dreadful, something which made Mr. Saunders come rushing back with a shout:

"Take her away! Take her to our apartment, Jennie. She must not see—"

Not see! He realized the futility of his words as his gaze fell on the young woman

who had risen up
at his approach and
now stood gazing at
him without speech,
without movement,
but with a glare of
terror in her eyes,
which gave him his
first realization of
human misery.

His own glance fell
before it. If he had
followed his instinct
he would have fled
the house rather than

answer the question of her look and the attitude of her whole frozen body.

Perhaps in mercy to his speechless terror, perhaps in mercy to herself, she was the one who at last found the word which voiced their mutual anguish.

"Dead?"

No answer. None was

needed.

"And my baby?"

O, that cry! It curdled the hearts of all who heard it. It shook the souls of men and women both inside and outside the apartment; then all was forgotten in the wild rush she made. The wife and mother had flung herself upon the scene, and, side by side with the not unmoved policeman, stood looking down upon the desolation made in one fatal instant in her home and heart.

They lay there together, both past help, both quite dead. The child had simply been strangled by the weight of his father's arm which lay directly across the upturned little throat. But the father was a victim of the shot they had heard. There was blood on his breast, and a pistol in his hand.

Suicide! The horrible truth was patent. No wonder they wanted to hold the young widow back. Her neighbour, Mrs. Saunders, crept in on tiptoe and put her arms about the swaying, fainting woman; but there was nothing to say—absolutely nothing.

At least, they thought not. But when they saw her throw herself down, not by her husband, but by the child, and drag it out from under that strangling arm and hug and kiss it and call out wildly for a doctor, the officer endeavoured to interfere and yet could not find the heart to do so, though he knew the child was dead and should not, according to all the rules of the coroner's office, be moved before that official arrived. Yet because no mother could be convinced of a fact like this, he let her sit with it on the floor and try all her little arts to revive it, while he gave orders to the janitor and waited himself for the arrival of doctor and coroner.

She was still sitting there in wide-eyed misery, alternately fondling the little body and drawing back to consult its small set features for some sign of life, when the doctor came, and, after one look at the child, drew it softly from her arms and laid it quietly in the crib from which its father had evidently lifted it but a short time before. Then he turned back to her, and found her on her feet, upheld by her two friends. She had understood his action, and without a groan had accepted her fate. Indeed, she seemed incapable of any further speech or action. She was staring down at her husband's body, which she, for the first time, seemed fully to see. Was her look one of grief or of resentment for the part he had played so unintentionally in her child's death? It was hard to tell;

and when, with slowly rising finger, she pointed to the pistol so tightly clutched in the other outstretched hand, no one there—and by this time the room was full—could foretell what her words would be when her tongue regained its usage and she could speak.

What she did say was

this:

"Is there a bullet gone? Did he fire off that pistol?" A question so manifestly one of delirium that no one answered it, which seemed to surprise her, though she said nothing till her glance had passed all around the walls of the room to where a window stood open to the night,—its lower sash being entirely raised. "There! look there!" she cried, with a commanding accent, and, throwing up her hands, sank a dead weight into the arms of those supporting her.

No one understood; but naturally more than one rushed to the window. An open

space was before
them. Here lay
the fields not yet
parcelled out into
lots and built upon;
but it was not upon
these they looked,
but upon the strong
trellis which they
found there, which, if
it supported no vine,
formed a veritable
ladder between this
window and the
ground.

Could she have meant to call attention to this fact; and were her words expressive of another idea than the obvious one of suicide?

If so, to what lengths a woman's imagination can go! Or so their combined looks seemed to proclaim, when to their utter astonishment they saw the officer, who had presented a calm appearance up till now, shift his position and with a surprised grunt direct their eyes to a portion of the wall just visible beyond the half-drawn curtains of the bed. The mirror hanging there showed a star-shaped breakage, such as follows the sharp impact of a bullet or a fiercely projected stone.

"He fired two shots. One went wild; the other straight home."

It was the officer delivering his opinion.

Mr. Saunders, returning from the distant room where he had assisted in carrying Mrs. Hammond, cast a look at the shattered glass, and remarked forcibly:

"I heard but one; and I was sitting up, disturbed by that poor infant. Jennie, did you hear more than one shot?" he asked, turning toward his wife.

"No," she answered, but not with the readiness he had evidently expected. "I heard only one, but that was not quite usual in its tone. I'm used to guns," she explained, turning to the officer. "My father was an army man, and he taught me very early to load and fire a pistol. There was a prolonged sound to this shot; something like an echo of itself, following close upon the first ping. Didn't you notice that,

Warren?"

"I remember something of the kind," her husband allowed.

"He shot twice and quickly," interposed the policeman, sententiously. "We shall find a spent bullet back of that mirror."

But when, upon the arrival of

the coroner, an investigation was made of the mirror and the wall behind, no bullet was found either there or any where else in the room, save in the dead man's breast. Nor had more than one been shot from his pistol, as five full chambers testified. The case which seemed so simple had its mysteries, but the assertion made by Mrs. Saunders no longer carried weight, nor was the evidence offered by the broken mirror considered as indubitably establishing the fact that a second shot had been fired in the room.

Yet it was equally evident that the charge which had

entered the dead speculator's breast had not been delivered at the close range of the pistol found clutched in his hand. There were no powder-marks to be discerned on his pajama-jacket, or on the flesh beneath. Thus anomaly confronted anomaly, leaving open but one other theory: that the bullet found in Mr. Hammond's breast came from the window and the one he shot went out of it. But this would necessitate his having shot his pistol from a point far removed from where he was found; and his wound was such as made it difficult to believe that he would stagger far, if at all, after its infliction.

Yet, because the
coroner was both
conscientious and
alert, he caused a
most rigorous search
to be made of the
ground overlooked by
the above mentioned
window; a search
in which the police
joined, but which
was without any
result save that of
rousing the attention
of people in the
neighbourhood and

leading to a story
being circulated of
a man seen some
time the night before
crossing the fields
in a great hurry.
But as no further
particulars were
forthcoming, and not
even a description of
the man to be had,
no emphasis would
have been laid upon
this story had it not
transpired that the
moment a report of

it had come to Mrs. Hammond's ears (why is there always some one to carry these reports?) she roused from the torpor into which she had fallen, and in wild fashion exclaimed:

"I knew it! I expected it! He was shot through the window and by that wretch. He never shot himself." Violent declarations which trailed off into the one continuous wail, “O, my baby! my poor baby!”

Such words, even though the fruit of delirium, merited some sort of attention, or so this good coroner thought, and as soon as opportunity offered and she was sufficiently sane and quiet to respond to his questions, he asked her whom she had meant by that wretch, and what reason she had, or thought she had, of attributing her husband's death to any other agency than his own disgust with life.

And then it was that his sympathies, although greatly

roused in her favour began to wane. She met the question with a cold stare followed by a few ambiguous words out of which he could make nothing. Had she said wretch? She did not remember. They must not be influenced by anything she might have uttered in her first grief. She was well-nigh insane at the time. But of one thing they might be sure: her husband had not shot himself; he was too much afraid of death for such an act. Besides, he was too happy. Whatever folks might say he was too fond of his family to wish to leave it.

Nor did the coroner or any other official succeed in eliciting anything further from her. Even when she was asked, with cruel insistence, how she explained the fact that the baby was found lying on the floor instead of in its crib, her only answer was: "His father was trying to soothe it. The child was crying dreadfully, as you have heard from those who were kept awake by him that night, and my husband was carrying him about when the shot came which caused George to fall and overlay the baby in his struggles."

"Carrying a baby about with a loaded pistol in his hand?" came back in stern retort.

She had no answer for this. She admitted when informed that

the bullet extracted from her husband's body had been found to correspond exactly with those remaining in the five chambers of the pistol taken from his hand, that he was not only the owner of this pistol but was in the habit of sleeping with it under his pillow; but, beyond that, nothing; and this reticence, as

well as her manner
which was cold
and repellent, told
against her.

A verdict of suicide
was rendered by the
coroner's jury, and
the life-insurance
company, in which
Mr. Hammond had but
lately insured himself
for a large sum,
taking advantage of
the suicide clause
embodied in the

policy, announced its determination of not paying the same.

Such was the situation, as known to Violet Strange and the general public, on the day she was asked to see Mrs. Hammond and learn what might alter her opinion as to the justice of this verdict and the stand taken by the Shuler Life

Insurance Company.

The clock on the mantel in Miss Strange's rose-coloured boudoir had struck three, and Violet was gazing in some impatience at the door, when there came a gentle knock upon it, and the maid (one of the elderly, not youthful, kind) ushered in her expected visitor.

"You are Mrs. Hammond?" she asked, in natural awe of the too black figure outlined so sharply against the deep pink of the sea-shell room.

The answer was a slow lifting of the veil which shadowed the features she knew only from the cuts she had seen in newspapers.

"You are—Miss Strange?" stammered her visitor; "the young lady who—"

"I am," chimed in a voice as ringing as it was sweet. "I am the person you have come here to see. And this is my home. But that does not make me less interested in the unhappy, or less desirous of serving them. Certainly you have met with the two greatest losses which can come to a woman—I know your story well enough to say that—; but what have you to tell me in proof that you should not lose your anticipated income as well? Something vital, I hope, else I cannot help you; something which you should have told the coroner's jury—and did not."

The flush which was the sole answer these words called forth did not take from the refinement of the young widow's expression, but rather added to it; Violet watched it in its ebb and flow and, seriously affected by it (why, she did not know, for Mrs.

Hammond had made no other appeal either by look or gesture), pushed forward a chair and begged her visitor to be seated.

"We can converse in perfect safety here," she said. "When you feel quite equal to it, let me hear what you have to communicate. It will never go any further. I could not do the work I do if I felt it necessary to have a confidant."

"But you are so young and so—so—"

"So inexperienced you would say and so evidently a member of what New Yorkers call 'society.' Do not let that trouble you. My inexperience is not likely to last long and my social pleasures are more apt to add to my efficiency than to detract from it."

With this Violet's face broke into a smile. It was not the brilliant one so often seen upon her lips, but there was something in its quality which carried encouragement to the widow and led her to say with obvious eagerness:

"You know the facts?"

"I have read all the papers."

"I was not believed on the stand."

"It was your manner—"

"I could not help my manner. I was keeping something back, and, being unused to deceit, I could not act quite naturally."

"Why did you keep something back? When you saw the unfavourable impression made by your reticence, why did you not speak up and frankly tell your story?"

"Because I was ashamed. Because I thought it would hurt me more to speak than to keep silent. I do not think so now; but I did then—and so made my great mistake. You must remember not only the awful shock of my double loss, but the sense of guilt accompanying it; for my husband and I had quarreled that night, quarreled bitterly—that was why I had run away into another room and not because I was feeling ill and impatient of the baby's fretful cries."

"So people have thought." In saying this, Miss Strange was perhaps cruelly emphatic. "You wish to explain that quarrel? You think it will be doing any good to your cause to go into that matter with me now?"

"I cannot say; but I

must first clear my conscience and then try to convince you that quarrel or no quarrel, he never took his own life. He was not that kind. He had an abnormal fear of death. I do not like to say it but he was a physical coward. I have seen him turn pale at the least hint of danger. He could no more have turned that muzzle upon his own breast than he could have turned it upon his baby. Some other hand shot him, Miss Strange. Remember the open window, the shattered mirror; and I think I know that hand."

Her head had fallen forward on her breast. The emotion she showed was not so eloquent of grief as of deep personal shame.

"You think you know the man?" In saying this, Violet's voice sunk to a whisper. It was an accusation of murder she had just heard.

"To my great distress, yes. When Mr. Hammond and I were married," the widow now proceeded in a more determined tone, "there was another man—a very violent one—who vowed even at the church door that George and I should never live out two full years together. We have not. Our second anniversary would have been in November."

"But—"

"Let me say this: the quarrel of which

I speak was not
serious enough to
occasion any such
act of despair on his
part. A man would be
mad to end his life on
account of so slight
a disagreement.
It was not even
on account of the
person of whom
I've just spoken,
though that person
had been mentioned
between us earlier
in the evening, Mr.

Hammond having come across him face to face that very afternoon in the subway. Up to this time neither of us had seen or heard of him since our wedding-day."

"And you think this person whom you barely mentioned, so mindful of his old grudge that he sought out your domicile, and, with the intention of murder, climbed the trellis leading to your room and turned his pistol upon the shadowy figure which was all he could see in the semi-obscurity of a much lowered gas-jet?"

"A man in the dark does not need a bright light to see his enemy when he is intent upon revenge."

Miss Strange altered her tone.

"And your husband? You must acknowledge that he shot off his pistol whether the other did or not."

"It was in self-defence. He would shoot to save his own life—or the baby's."

"Then he must have heard or seen—"

"A man at the window."

"And would have shot there?"

"Or tried to."

"Tried to?"

"Yes; the other shot first—oh, I've thought it all out—causing my husband's bullet to go wild. It was his which broke the mirror."

Violet's eyes, bright as stars, suddenly narrowed.

"And what happened then?" she asked. "Why cannot they find the bullet?"

"Because it went out of the window;—glanced off and went out of the window."

Mrs. Hammond's tone was triumphant; her look spirited and intense.

Violet eyed her compassionately.

"Would a bullet glancing off from a mirror, however hung, be apt to reach a window so far on the opposite side?"

"I don't know; I only know that it did," was

the contradictory, almost absurd, reply.

"What was the cause of the quarrel you speak of between your husband and yourself? You see, I must know the exact truth and all the truth to be of any assistance to you."

"It was—it was about the care I gave, or didn't give, the baby. I feel awfully to have to say it, but George did not think I did my full duty by the child. He said there was no need of its crying so; that if I gave it the proper attention it would not keep the neighbours and himself awake half the night. And I—I got angry and insisted that I did the best I could; that the child was naturally fretful and that if he wasn't satisfied with my way of looking after it, he might try his. All of which was very wrong and unreasonable on my part, as witness the awful punishment which followed."

"And what made you get up and leave him?"

"The growl he gave me in reply. When I heard that, I bounded

out of bed and said
I was going to the
spare room to sleep;
and if the baby cried
he might just try
what he could do
himself to stop it."

"And he answered?"

"This, just this—I
shall never forget
his words as long as
I live—'If you go, you
need not expect me
to let you in again
no matter what

happens.'"

"He said that?"

"And locked the door after me. You see I could not tell all that."

"It might have been better if you had. It was such a natural quarrel and so unprovocative of actual tragedy."

Mrs. Hammond was

silent. It was not difficult to see that she had no very keen regrets for her husband personally. But then he was not a very estimable man nor in any respect her equal.

"You were not happy with him," Violet ventured to remark.

"I was not a fully contented woman. But for all that

he had no cause
to complain of
me except for
the reason I have
mentioned. I was not
a very intelligent
mother. But if the
baby were living
now—O, if he were
living now—with what
devotion I should
care for him."

She was on her feet,
her arms were raised,
her face impassioned

with feeling. Violet, gazing at her, heaved a little sigh. It was perhaps in keeping with the situation, perhaps extraneous to it, but whatever its source, it marked a change in her manner. With no further check upon her sympathy, she said very softly:

"It is well with the child."

The mother stiffened,

swayed, and then burst into wild weeping.

"But not with me," she cried, "not with me. I am desolate and bereft. I have not even a home in which to hide my grief and no prospect of one."

"But," interposed Violet, "surely your husband left you something? You cannot be quite penniless?"

"My husband left nothing," was the answer, uttered without bitterness, but with all the hardness of fact. "He had debts. I shall pay those debts. When these and other necessary expenses are liquidated, there will be but little left. He made no secret of the fact that he lived close up to his means. That is why he was induced to take on a life insurance. Not a friend of his but knows his improvidence. I—I have not even jewels. I have only my determination and an absolute conviction as to the real nature of my husband's death."

"What is the name of the man you secretly believe to have shot your husband from the trellis?"

Mrs. Hammond told her.

It was a new one to Violet. She said so and then asked:

"What else can you tell me about him?"

"Nothing, but that he

is a very dark man and has a club-foot."

"Oh, what a mistake you've made."

"Mistake? Yes, I acknowledge that."

"I mean in not giving this last bit of information at once to the police. A man can be identified by such a defect. Even his footsteps can be traced. He might have been found that very day. Now, what have we to go upon?"

"You are right, but not expecting to have any difficulty about the insurance money I thought it would be generous in me to keep still. Besides, this is only surmise on my part. I feel certain that my husband was shot by another hand than his own, but I know of no way of proving it. Do you?"

Then Violet talked seriously with her, explaining how their only hope lay in the discovery of a second bullet in the room which had already been ransacked for this very purpose and without the shadow of a result.

A tea, a musicale, and an evening dance kept Violet Strange in a whirl for the remainder of the day. No brighter eye nor more contagious wit lent brilliance to these occasions, but with the passing of the midnight hour no one who had seen her in the blaze of electric lights would have recognized this favoured child of fortune in the earnest figure sitting in the obscurity of an up-town apartment, studying the walls, the ceilings, and the floors by the dim light of a lowered gas-jet. Violet Strange in society was a very different person from Violet Strange under the tension of her secret and peculiar work.

She had told them at home that she was going to spend the night with a friend; but only her old coachman knew who that friend was. Therefore a very natural sense of guilt mingled with her emotions at finding herself alone on a scene whose gruesome mystery she could solve only by identifying herself with the place and the man who had perished there.

Dismissing from her mind all thought of self, she strove to think as he thought, and act as he acted on the night when he found himself (a man of but little courage) left in this room with an ailing child.

At odds with himself, his wife, and possibly

with the child
screaming away in
its crib, what would
he be apt to do in his
present emergency?
Nothing at first, but
as the screaming
continued he would
remember the old
tales of fathers
walking the floor
at night with crying
babies, and hasten to
follow suit. Violet, in
her anxiety to reach
his inmost thought,

crossed to where the crib had stood, and, taking that as a start, began pacing the room in search of the spot from which a bullet, if shot, would glance aside from the mirror in the direction of the window. (Not that she was ready to accept this theory of Mrs. Hammond, but that she did not wish to entirely dismiss it without putting it to the test.)

She found it in an unexpected quarter of the room and much nearer the bed-head than where his body was found. This, which might seem to confuse matters, served, on the contrary to remove from the case one of its most serious difficulties. Standing here, he was within reach of the pillow under which his pistol lay hidden, and if startled, as his wife believed him to have been by a noise at the other end of the room, had but to crouch and reach behind him in order to find himself armed and ready for a possible intruder.

Imitating his action

in this as in other things, she had herself crouched low at the bedside and was on the point of withdrawing her hand from under the pillow, when a new surprise checked her movement and held her fixed in her position, with eyes staring straight at the adjoining wall. She had seen there what he must have seen in making this same turn—the dark bars of the opposite window-frame outlined in the mirror—and understood at once what had happened. In the nervousness and terror of the moment, George Hammond had mistaken this reflection of the window for the window itself, and

shot impulsively
at the man he
undoubtedly saw
covering him from the
trellis without. But
while this explained
the shattering of the
mirror, how about
the other and still
more vital question,
of where the bullet
went afterward? Was
the angle at which
it had been fired
acute enough to send
it out of a window

diagonally opposed? No; even if the pistol had been held closer to the man firing it than she had reason to believe, the angle still would be oblique enough to carry it on to the further wall.

But no sign of any such impact had been discovered on this wall. Consequently, the force of the bullet had been expended before reaching it, and when it fell—

Here, her glance, slowly traveling along the floor, impetuously paused. It had reached the spot where the two bodies had been found, and unconsciously her eyes rested there, conjuring up the picture of the bleeding father and

the strangled child.
How piteous and
how dreadful it all
was. If she could
only understand—
Suddenly she rose
straight up, staring
and immovable
in the dim light.
Had the idea—the
explanation—the
only possible
explanation covering
the whole phenomena
come to her at last?

It would seem
so, for as she so
stood, a look of
conviction settled
over her features,
and with this look,
evidences of a horror
which for all her
fast accumulating
knowledge of life and
its possibilities made
her appear very small
and very helpless.

A half-hour later,
when Mrs. Hammond,

in her anxiety at hearing nothing more from Miss Strange, opened the door of her room, it was to find, lying on the edge of the sill, the little detective's card with these words hastily written across it:

I do not feel as well as I could wish, and so have telephoned to my own coachman to come and take me home. I will either see or write you within a few days. But do not allow yourself to hope. I pray you do not allow yourself the least hope; the outcome is still very problematical.

When Violet's employer entered his office the next morning it was to find a veiled figure awaiting him which he at once recognized as that of his little deputy. She was slow in lifting her veil and when it finally came free he felt a momentary doubt as to his wisdom in giving her just such a matter as this to investigate. He was quite sure of his mistake when he saw her face, it was so drawn and pitiful.

"You have failed," said he.

"Of that you must judge," she answered; and drawing near she whispered in his ear.

"No!" he cried in his amazement.

"Think," she murmured, "think. Only so can all the facts be accounted for."

“I will look into it; I will certainly look into it,” was his earnest reply. “If you are right—But never mind that. Go home and take a horseback ride in the Park. When I have news in regard to this I will let you know. Till then forget it all. Hear me, I charge you to forget everything but your balls and your parties."

And Violet obeyed him.

Some few days after this, the following statement appeared in all the papers:

"Owing to some remarkable work done by the firm of —— & ——, the well-known private detective agency, the claim made by Mrs.

George Hammond against the Shuler Life Insurance Company is likely to be allowed without further litigation. As our readers will remember, the contestant has insisted from the first that the bullet causing her husband's death came from another pistol than the one found clutched in his own hand. But while reasons were not lacking to substantiate this assertion, the failure to discover more than the disputed track of a second bullet led to a verdict of suicide, and a refusal of the company to pay.

"But now that bullet has been found. And where? In the most startling place in the

world, viz.: in the
larynx of the child
found lying dead
upon the floor beside
his father, strangled
as was supposed
by the weight of
that father's arm.
The theory is, and
there seems to be
none other, that
the father, hearing
a suspicious noise
at the window, set
down the child he
was endeavouring

to soothe and made for the bed and his own pistol, and, mistaking a reflection of the assassin for the assassin himself, sent his shot sidewise at a mirror just as the other let go the trigger which drove a similar bullet into his breast. The course of the one was straight and fatal and that of the other deflected. Striking the mirror

at an oblique angle,
the bullet fell to the
floor where it was
picked up by the
crawling child, and,
as was most natural,
thrust at once into
his mouth. Perhaps it
felt hot to the little
tongue; perhaps the
child was simply
frightened by some
convulsive movement
of the father who
evidently spent
his last moment in

an endeavour to reach the child, but, whatever the cause, in the quick gasp it gave, the bullet was drawn into the larynx, strangling him.

"That the father's arm, in his last struggle, should have fallen directly across the little throat is one of those anomalies which confounds reason and misleads justice by stopping investigation at the very point where truth lies and mystery disappears.

"Mrs. Hammond is to be congratulated that there are detectives who do not give too much credence to outward appearances."

We expect soon to hear of the capture

of the man who sped home the death-dealing bullet.

ABOUT THE AUTHOR

In 1887, a decade before Sherlock Holmes, Anna Katharine Green wrote her first detective story and began her genre defining career. Born in Brooklyn in 1846, she defied a male dominated field and pioneered many conventions of mysteries that remain today.

ABOUT THE COVER

The image on the cover is adapted from a lithograph by the Austrian-Czech artist Alphonse Mucha entitled, “Flirt”. It was made sometime between 1895-1900.

VIOLET STRANGE RETURNS IN AN INTANGIBLE CLUE

MORE BOOKS AT:

superlargeprint.com

KEEP ON READING!

This book is set in a font designed by Abelardo Gonzalez called OpenDyslexic

ISBN 9781088801772

Printed in Great Britain
by Amazon

39957373R00081